LOVELAND PUBLIC LIBRARY
000369239

D0923168

To Becky and Lisa – E.J.

With love to Michael – husband, friend, partner, and my double in many, many ways – D.O.B.

Gifted & Talented® is an imprint of Lowell House Juvenile,
a division of RGA Publishing Group, Inc.

Publisher: Jack Artenstein
General Manager: Elizabeth Duell Wood
Editorial Director: Brenda Pope-Ostrow
Director of Publishing Services: Mary D. Aarons
Text Design: Anne Richardson-Daniel
Cover Design: Lisa-Theresa Lenthall

Manufactured in the United States of America

ISBN: 1-56565-162-6

Library of Congress Catalog Card Number: 94-29254

10 9 8 7 6 5 4 3 2 1

A GIFTED & TALENTED® READER • AGES 6-8

Double the Trouble

By Ellen Javernick, M.Ed.
Illustrated by Dianne O'Quinn Burke

To Brad,
Love, Ellen Javernick

Lowell House
Juvenile
Los Angeles

CONTEMPORARY BOOKS
Chicago

NOTE TO PARENTS:

This **GIFTED & TALENTED® READER** is not like any other reader. It is an interactive picture book. By "interactive" we mean that your child will not be a passive listener but will become a participant in the learning process. The questions provided will encourage your child to discuss, reason, and reflect, as well as read! This **GIFTED & TALENTED® READER** has been designed for you to read with your child, for your child to later read on his or her own, and even for the child to read to you! It will open your child's mind to a love of reading and will help fulfill his or her true potential.

On the next page you will find some examples of the kinds of open-ended questions you can use to elicit responses from your child. Picture books are written to be read many times, so ask just one or two questions each time you read the story with your child. You can listen to your child's answers and let the creative dialogue take off from there.

Each question is based on one or more specific critical and creative thinking skills. These skills of logic and reasoning teach children **how to think,** and they are precisely the skills emphasized by teachers of gifted and talented children. If a child has a grasp of how to think, school success will become more assured, and your child will become self-confident as he or she approaches new tasks with the ability to think them through. Here are some of the skills being emphasized:

- **Deduction** - the ability to reach a logical conclusion by interpreting clues
- **Understanding Relationships** - the ability to recognize similarities or dissimilarities; to classify and categorize
- **Sequencing** - the ability to organize events, numbers; to recognize patterns
- **Inference** - the ability to reach a logical conclusion from given or assumed evidence
- **Creative Thinking** - the ability to generate unique ideas; to compare and contrast the same elements in different situations; to present imaginative solutions to problems

GIFTED & TALENTED® READERS are educationally sound and endorsed by leaders in the gifted field. They will benefit *any* child who is just beginning to read; who demonstrates curiosity, imagination, a sense of fun and wonder about the world, and a desire to learn.

Questions to Stimulate Critical and Creative Thinking Skills:

- What did Mr. and Mrs. Witherspoon say when they took the girls somewhere? Do you think the girls did what their parents told them to do?
- How could you tell that Mr. and Mrs. Witherspoon really thought having twins was fun?
- Do you think the girls will always be "double the trouble"?
- What clues did the Witherspoons have to help them find Rosie and Violet? How did they know which twin was which?
- Did you know where Rosie and Violet would be? Did you follow any of the clues in the story?
- Why do you think it would be fun to have a twin brother or sister? Why not?
- There are a few different signs in this book. Do you remember where they are?
- The Witherspoons went to four different places. Where did they go first? After that? Where did they go last? You can use the changes in the seasons to help you remember.
- Can you name five or more things you might see at each of the places the Witherspoons visited?
- Where could **you** be found at each of those places?
- At one point in the story, the Witherspoons found Rosie **bathing in the birdbath**. The words **bathing** and **birdbath** start with the same sound. Sometimes writers put two or more words with the same sound close together. Can you find more groups of words in the story that are close together and start with the same sound?
- How are Rosie and Violet the same? How are they different? Think of as many ways as you can.

When the twins were born, Mrs. Witherspoon was very happy. But her friends told her, "Twins are double the trouble."

Mr. Witherspoon looked at his matching baby girls. He smiled. “How will we tell them apart?” he asked.

“Do not worry,” Mrs. Witherspoon said. “We can name them Rosie and Violet. Rosie will always wear pink. Violet will always wear purple.”

Mr. and Mrs. Witherspoon painted the twins' room. They used pretty pink and purple paint. They bought the girls lots of pink and purple toys.

For a while, it was not hard to tell them apart. Life was peaceful for the family. But Rosie and Violet got bigger. And so did the Witherspoons' troubles!

First Rosie would not wear pink. Then Violet would not wear purple. The twins wanted to wear matching clothes. Mr. and Mrs. Witherspoon had a problem. They could not tell which twin was which!

Next the girls started going in opposite directions. The Witherspoons learned to follow clues. The clues helped them find the twins.

One summer day Mrs. Witherspoon took Rosie and Violet shopping. They went to Super Sport to buy swimsuits.

Rosie picked a swimsuit with polkadots. Violet picked one with ruffles.

Mrs. Witherspoon got in line to pay. "You may look around," she said. "But stay near me. And stay out of trouble."

The girls went off in opposite directions.

The store clerk gave Mrs. Witherspoon her bag. Then she began to look for the twins.

Another mother said, “Seems like twins are double the trouble.” Mrs. Witherspoon just smiled.

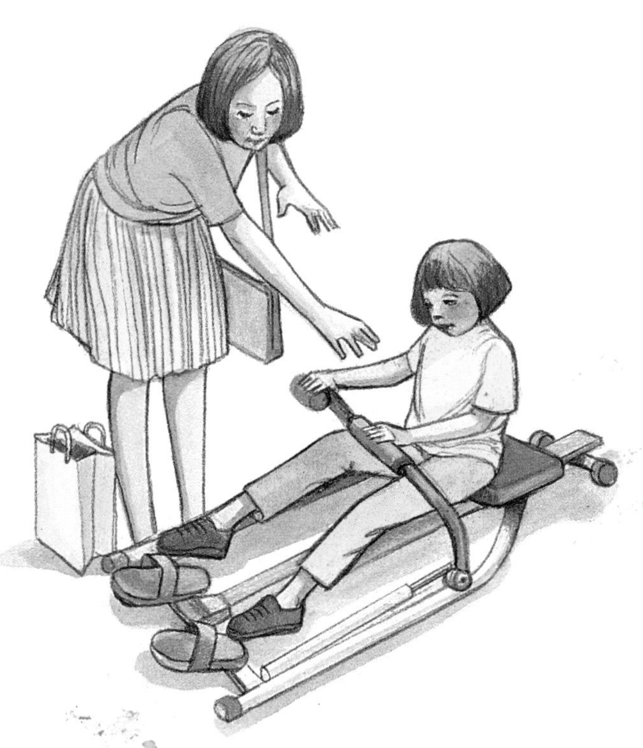

She found Violet first. Violet was riding on a rowing machine. Mrs. Witherspoon took her hand. Together they looked for Rosie.

They saw Rosie at last. She waved at them from the wall. Rosie had climbed high up the climbing wall.

"Get down!" Mrs. Witherspoon said. "It is time to go."

One day in the fall Mr. Witherspoon took the twins out. They went to the school carnival.

"I want to go in the Spooky House," said Rosie.

"I want to get my face painted," said Violet.

"I have to help blow up balloons," said their dad. "You may do what you like. But stay out of trouble."

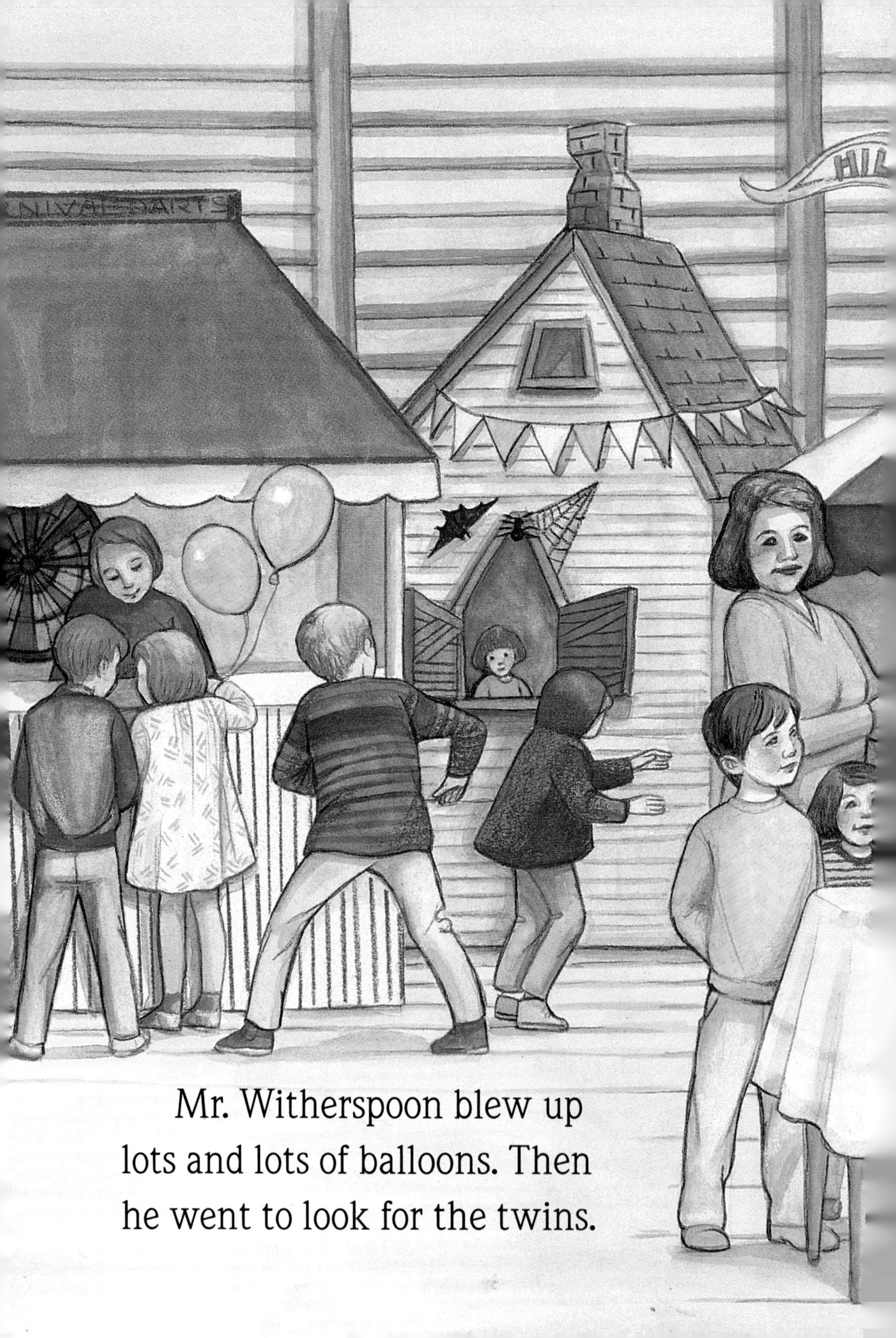

Mr. Witherspoon blew up lots and lots of balloons. Then he went to look for the twins.

SIDE SCHOOL

Mr. Witherspoon heard a scream in the Spooky House. He knew it was Rosie.

He found Violet making monkey faces in a mirror.

The principal patted him on the shoulder. “Twins can be double the trouble,” she said.

One cold winter day Mrs. Witherspoon took Rosie and Violet to Pet Town. "The birds can not find food in the snow," she said. "We must buy them some birdseed."

"I want to look at the puppies," said Violet.

"And the hamster," said Rosie.

"You may do both," said their mom. "But stay out of trouble."

Mrs. Witherspoon paid for a big bag of birdseed. She started to look for the twins. Then she saw her friend Myrna.

"I will help you find the girls," said Myrna.

“Look,” said Myrna. “Is that one of your girls? She is playing in the puppy pen.”

“It is Violet,” said Mrs. Witherspoon. “And I bet I know where Rosie is!” Mrs. Witherspoon helped Violet out of the pen. Then all three of them hurried to the hamster’s cage.

Rosie was not there. The hamster was not there!

Just then the hamster hopped by. Rosie came hurrying after it. "Help!" called Rosie.

They soon caught the hamster. Then Myrna said, "I told you twins could be double the trouble."

Mrs. Witherspoon sighed. She waved good-bye to Myrna.

In the spring the Witherspoons went to the Garden Center. The twins' dad looked at bags and bags of dirt.

"This is boring," said Rosie.

"I want to see the colorful flowers," said Violet.

"You may look around," said their mom. "Just stay near me. And stay out of trouble." Rosie and Violet skipped off.

Mr. Witherspoon took a long time to find the best dirt. It took even more time to find the girls.

Mr. Witherspoon saw Violet. She was tiptoeing through the tulips.

"I like these pretty flowers," Violet said.

Mrs. Witherspoon found Rosie bathing in a birdbath. "Peep, peep, peep," said Rosie.

Mrs. Witherspoon put the girls in the car.

Mr. Witherspoon put the bags of dirt in the car.

"Your friends were right," Mr. Witherspoon said quietly. "Twins can be double the trouble."

One night, just for fun, Rosie put on Violet's nightgown. Violet put on Rosie's P.J.s. Then they jumped into each other's beds.

Mr. Witherspoon did not know who he was hugging. Mrs. Witherspoon did not know who she was kissing.

“Surprise!” shouted Rosie and Violet. They started to giggle.

“Twins may be double the trouble,” Mrs. Witherspoon said. “But they are twice as much fun!”

Mr. Witherspoon laughed and laughed.